Small-Town Charm

COLORING BOOK

TERESA GOODRIDGE

DOVER PUBLICATIONS
GARDEN CITY, NEW YORK

Need a break from the everyday hustle and bustle? The 31 charming illustrations in this coloring book will transport you to the cozy and calm small-town life that's sure to be the perfect remedy. Take a leisurely walk past farm stands, general stores, and antique shops. Then stop by the café for a homemade treat—and don't forget to say hello to the friendly animals along the way! The artwork is printed on one side only, and the pages are perforated for easy removal and display.

Small-Town Charm Coloring Book is a new work, first published by Dover Publications in 2024.

ISBN-13: 978-0-486-85402-1
ISBN-10: 0-486-85402-7

Publisher: Betina Cochran
Managing Editorial Supervisor: Susan Rattiner
Production Editor: Gregory Koutrouby
Cover Designer: Peter Donahue
Creative Manager and Interior Designer: Marie Zaczkiewicz
Production: Pam Weston, Tammi McKenna, Ayse Yilmaz

Manufactured in the United States of America
85402701   2024
www.doverpublications.com

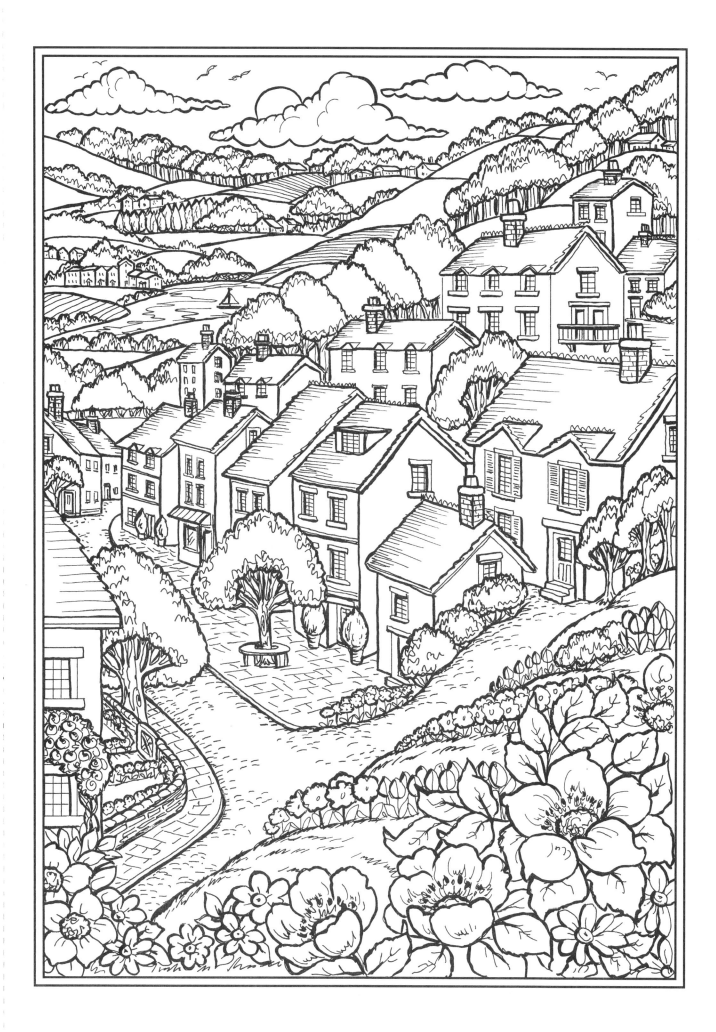